THE JUNGLE BOOK

Abridged by Joyce McAleer
Illustrated by Diana Catchpole

CARNIVAL

There are two Jungle Books and between them they contain many wonderful stories about the ways and laws of the jungle creatures and their exciting adventures.

Some of the best-known and best-loved of these stories are about an unusual jungle creature – not an animal, but a human boy!

A STRANGE NEW CUB!

The story starts with a family of wolves who lived in India. Their home was a cave in the hills and like all wolves, they had to hunt for their food.

One very warm, moonlit evening, Father Wolf, who had been resting, turned to Mother Wolf, who was lying with her four squealing, playful cubs. "It is time to hunt again," he said.

"Good luck go with you, O Chief of the Wolves," came a voice. It was Tabaqui, the jackal. The wolves weren't very pleased to see him because he was always telling tales and making mischief.

"Shere Khan, the big, fierce tiger with a lame foot, is hunting in these hills tonight," said the jackal, as he helped himself to a bone belonging to the wolves.

Father Wolf was angry, "By the law of the jungle, Shere Khan has no right to change his hunting-grounds without warning us."

Tabaqui greedily chewed the meat from the bone.

"Get out from our cave!" ordered Father Wolf.

"Listen, can't you hear Shere Khan?" asked the sly, spiteful jackal, as he left.

Sure enough, a terrible whine could be heard, followed by a loud howl.

"He has charged and missed," said Mother Wolf. A rustling sound came from the bushes outside. "Something is coming up the hill."

Father wolf got ready to pounce, but stopped himself quickly, and just stared in astonishment at the sight before him.

It was a little naked baby boy, with soft, dimpled skin. He looked up and laughed at Father Wolf.

"I've never seen a man's cub before," said Mother Wolf. "Bring it here."

Father Wolf gently carried the child in his mouth without even leaving a scratch. Unafraid, the baby snuggled up to Mother Wolf's warm coat.

"Was there ever a wolf who could boast of a man's cub among her children?" she asked proudly.

"I've heard of it," answered Father Wolf, "but not in our Pack or in my time."

Then, suddenly, the moonlight was blocked from the mouth of the cave as Shere Khan thrust in his huge head and shoulders. Tabaqui, the jackal, was behind the great tiger squeaking, "It went in there."

"Shere Khan, why do you come here?" asked Father Wolf.

"A man's cub came this way. Its parents have run off. Give it to me!"

"The man's cub is ours now," said Father Wolf.

The fierce tiger was too big to get right into the cave, but he roared like thunder.

Mother Wolf sprang forward to face the blazing eyes of Shere Khan, her eyes shone like two green

moons in the darkness. "The man's cub will stay here," she cried. "He will run with the Pack and hunt with the Pack."

Shere Khan was afraid of Mother Wolf, so he backed off, growling, "Let's just see what the rest of the Pack say about it! The man's cub will be mine in the end, you'll see!"

Mother Wolf gazed down fondly at her strange new cub. "Lie still," she murmured. "I must give you a name. I know, I'll call you Mowgli."

Father Wolf looked on, worried. He knew that Shere Khan was right: the baby must be shown to the Pack. Would they be allowed to keep him as their own?

THE PACK DECIDES

It was a law of the jungle that as soon as wolf cubs were old enough to stand on their feet, they had to be brought to the Pack Council. This was held once a month on the night of the full moon at a place called Council Rock, a hilltop covered with stones and boulders.

Akela, the Pack's leader, lay on his rock and below him sat more than forty wolves of every size and colour. The senior wolves inspected each cub in turn. At last they came to little Mowgli, who sat laughing and playing with pebbles.

From behind the rocks came the muffled roar of Shere Khan crying, "That cub is mine! Give him to me! Wolves don't need a man's cub!"

A young wolf echoed Shere Khan's cry. "We don't want a man's cub!"

"Who speaks for this cub?" asked Akela.

The law of the jungle said that, in order to be accepted, a new cub must be spoken for by at least two members of the Pack. Father and Mother Wolf kept silent, for their votes didn't count.

No sound came from the wolves. Mother Wolf's heart sank; would no-one speak?

Now there was one other creature who was allowed to attend the Pack Council – Baloo, the sleepy brown bear. He came and went as he pleased, because he ate only nuts, roots and honey. He also taught the wolf cubs the law of the jungle.

He rose up on his hind legs and grunted, "I speak for the man's cub. Let him stay and run with the Pack. I will teach him everything he needs to know."

"Baloo has spoken, but we need another. Who else will speak for this cub?" asked Akela.

A shadow fell over the circle of wolves. It was Bagheera, the sleek, inky-black panther. He was a feared creature – cunning and bold, with a silky-soft coat and a voice as sweet as honey.

"I know that I have no right to be here," he purred, "but jungle law states that the life of a cub may be bought at a price. Is that right?"

"Quite right," cried the wolves.

"It'd be a shame to kill this man's cub, so if you accept him, I will let you have a bull I've just killed. The bull is very fat and tasty."

The hungry wolves smacked their lips and agreed at once. "What does it matter?" they said. "The man's cub won't last long in the jungle, anyway! He will die in the winter rains. He will burn in the sun. What harm can he do us?"

All this time, the little boy went on playing with the pebbles. The wolves looked closely at him, then made their way down the hill towards the bull. Shere Khan roared in anger.

Akela turned to Father Wolf, "Take the man's cub and train him as one of us."

That was how Mowgli came to be part of the Pack – on the word of Baloo the bear, and for the price of a bull.

GROWING UP IN THE JUNGLE!

Mowgli led a wonderful life among the wolves. He played with the other cubs and learned all about the ways of the jungle. The wolves were his family. He loved them and they loved him. Baloo taught him lots of things and Bagheera the panther was also very kind to him.

Mowgli spent long, happy days learning, climbing, resting in the sun and swimming in the pools. Baloo told him that honey and nuts were just as good to eat as raw meat.

Soon Mowgli could swing through the branches of the trees almost as well as the apes and he knew how to tell a sound branch from an unsafe one. He learned what to say if he disturbed a hive of wild bees or Mang the Bat – and how to warn the water snakes before splashing down on them when he went swimming.

He also had to learn the stranger's hunting call. This was used by a jungle creature hunting outside his own grounds. It meant, "Let me hunt here because I'm hungry", and the answer was, "Very well. But hunt for food, not for pleasure."

Like any child, Mowgli sometimes got tired of his lessons and then Baloo would be cross. Bagheera, who spoiled the little boy, told Baloo to be more gentle.

"There is nothing too little to be killed in the jungle," replied the wise bear. "That's why I teach him everything and smack him very softly when he is bad. It's for his own good. I'm teaching him all the master words of the jungle, so that he can protect himself. I'll ask him to say them for you."

Mowgli had run off in a temper and was sulking and hiding in a tree, but he was always delighted to show off, so he slid down the trunk. "I know all the master words," he said proudly, as he recited the special calls for the kite bird and the snake-people.

Mowgli was excited and very pleased with himself. He climbed on Bagherra's back and jumped up and down, clapping his hands and making faces. "The monkey-people said I'm their brother except that I have no tail! They're good to me and give me nuts and they don't hit me with hard paws. The monkeys play all day long!"

Baloo and Bagheera were both shocked and angry to hear this.

"Listen man-cub," said the big brown bear. "I've taught you all the laws of the jungle-people, except those of the monkeys, because they have no law. All they do is laugh and chatter; they have no speech of their own, only stolen words. We have no dealings

with them, and neither must you."

Now what Baloo said was true. The monkey-people or Bandar-log as they were known, lived in the tree tops and ran around fighting and laughing and shrieking among themselves. They'd throw sticks at the other animals and would even torment a wounded wolf or tiger just for fun.

They had no leader or customs of their own, but they had been watching Mowgli make little huts out of fallen branches. How useful he would be in their tribe!

STOLEN BY THE MONKEYS

The sly monkey-people saw Mowgli lying between Baloo and Bagheera as all three enjoyed a midday nap. Wasting no time, they grabbed him with hard, strong hands and pulled him up from where he lay. With great speed they carried him through the tree-tops. Baloo growled deeply and Bagheera tried to leap up the tree trunks, but it was no use.

"All the jungle-people will admire us for our skill and cunning!" yelled the monkeys in triumph.

Far down below, the still green jungle stretched for miles and poor Mowgli felt sick and giddy. The branches and leaves lashed at him as he was carried along the lower limbs of the trees. So they went, up and down and through the trees, bounding and crashing and whooping and screaming.

High in the blue sky, Mowgli saw Chil, the kite. The bird noticed that the monkeys were carrying something and flew closer to look.

Then Mowgli had an idea: he gave the kite call Baloo had taught him, and shouted, "Mark my trail. I'm Mowgli, the man-cub. Tell Baloo and Bagheera. . ."

The bear and panther were full of grief and fury at the loss of their young friend.

"Unless the monkeys drop him, the man-cub should be alright," said Baloo. "He is wise and clever, and he can frighten jungle creatures just by looking into their eyes. But the monkeys aren't afraid of anything. . ." Then he roared, "Oh, what a fool I am! There *is* someone they are terrified of – Kaa, the rock snake. We'll seek his help."

They found Kaa stretched out in the warm
afternoon sun. He had a beautiful new skin, so he was
very pleased with himself and twisted his thirty-foot
long body into fantastic knots and curves. He wasn't a
poisonous snake, but he had enormous strength and
power.

"We are hunting," said Baloo.

"Let me come with you," said Kaa. "But I must be
careful; these branches aren't what they were when I
was young. On my last hunt I slipped and waked the
Bander-log and they called me evil names. . ."

"They call you footless, yellow earthworm," said
Bagheera under his whiskers. "And they say that
you've lost all your teeth."

"Ssss! How dare they say such things!" hissed the snake, trying not to show how furious he was.

"The monkeys have taken our man-cub," said Baloo.

"Which way did they go with him?" asked the angry snake.

Suddenly there came a voice from above, "Baloo! Baloo!" It was Chil, the kite, with Mowgli's message.

"The monkeys have taken the man-cub to the Cold Lairs," called the bird.

"We must go there and rescue him straight away," said Bagheera.

IN THE LOST CITY

The Cold Lairs was a deserted city which had been built by a king in ancient times. Now the once-great palace was roofless, the marble fountains were split and grass sprouted up in the courtyard where the king's elephants were housed. To the monkey-people it was *their* city. They ran in and out of the ruins, pretending to be men.

Mowgli was tired, hungry and miserable. He tried to sleep but the monkeys joined hands and danced around singing silly songs. He asked for food and some monkeys went to get him some nuts but they soon forgot and fell down fighting instead.

The weary boy walked towards the city walls, but the monkeys pulled him back and pinched his skin, saying how lucky he was to be with them and how happy he should be.

"We're great! We're free! We're wonderful! It must be true, because we say so!" yelled the monkeys.

They were just so silly that Mowgli couldn't help smiling at them. "Do they never go to sleep?" he asked himself.

Meanwhile, Bagheera and Kaa had arrived at Cold Lairs. Baloo was following, as he couldn't travel as fast. Without a sound, Bagheera spotted Mowgli and crept up to the monkeys who surrounded him. Like a streak of lightning he struck at them. A scuffling mass of monkeys closed in on the panther, biting and scratching him, while others took hold of Mowgli. They dragged him through a hole in the dome of a summer-house which had been built for queens of long ago.

"Stay there," shouted the monkeys, "and we'll play with you later – if the poison-people don't kill you first!"

"Ssss! Hissss!" Mowgli knew these sounds even in the darkness. The summer-house was alive with cobras or 'poison-people'. Luckily Baloo had taught him the special call for protection, so they didn't attack him.

Mowgli watched Bagheera through some slits in the summer-house walls. "Get to the water!" he screamed to his friend. "You'll be safe there!"

At once Bagheera hurled himself into some old water tanks where the monkeys couldn't follow.

At that moment Baloo arrived but he immediately disappeared from sight beneath scores of screeching monkeys. High above flew Mang the Bat carrying news of the terrible fight he had just seen.

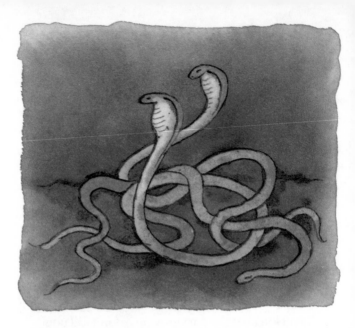

But the monkeys had not won yet. Kaa was hidden in the undergrowth, watching and waiting for his moment. Suddenly he struck! He delivered his first blow at the group of monkeys attacking Baloo. They offered no resistance and soon it was all over. Terrified, the monkeys ran as fast as they could from their old enemy.

Kaa went to the summer house. "Stand back, manling, and watch out, poison-people, while I break down the wall!"

Lifting his great body clear of the ground, Kaa sent six blows, nose-first into the wall. Mowgli was free!

TIME TO GO

Mowgli grew bigger and stronger daily. He went hunting with Bagheera, who told him that he must never hunt cattle, as his life was bought for the price of a bull. Mother Wolf warned him to beware of Shere Khan and to kill him one day. He also took his place at the Council Rock.

"Akela is old. He won't lead the Pack for much longer," said Bagheera. "Shere Khan has taught them that a man's cub doesn't belong with wolves. Soon you will be a man."

"But the wolves are my brothers," said Mowgli.

"I was born in captivity," the panther explained. "I escaped back to the jungle but I know the ways of men. That is why not even I can look straight into your eyes, although I love you dearly. Just as I went back to where I belonged, so must you, or you may be killed at the next Council. Get the red flower for protection."

Red flower was the name that jungle creatures gave to fire, which terrified the wolves. Mowgli ran fast down to the village huts and took a pot of burning charcoal away with him.

That night he attended the Council. Shere Khan spoke to the pack, saying, "The man's cub has lived too long. Give him to me."

"A man! A man!" snarled the angry wolves in agreement.

Old Akela begged for Mowgli's life but none listened. Desperately the boy held the fire high above him. The wolves cowered in fright.

"I will leave," said Mowgli. "And when I return as a man, it will be with Shere Khan's hide. Do not harm Akela. He was always my friend."

Mowgli looked around at the few wolves who'd been on his side, and then he felt a terrible hurt inside and tears filled his eyes. It was the first time he had cried and he was bewildered.

"Am I dying, Bagheera?" he asked.

"No, little brother," replied the panther. "It is only men's tears. Let them fall, Mowgli. They are just tears."

So Mowgli sat and cried as though his heart would break. Then he knew it was time to go.

He bade farewell to Mother and Father Wolf. "Don't forget me," he said.

"Little naked son, child of man, I'll always love you," replied Mother Wolf softly and with a heavy heart.

AMONG MEN

Mowgli didn't want to stay in the nearest village – it was too close to the jungle, so he kept walking until he came to another one. The people there stared at him, and, of course, he couldn't speak their language.

Some women examined him. "Poor child," they said.

Then one woman said to another, "He looks a bit like the boy you lost, Messua."

The woman wasn't sure, but took him to her hut and gave him bread and milk. Being indoors made Mowgli feel trapped. He also hated sleeping in a bed, so that night he crept out and lay down in the field.

Suddenly, a soft nose poked him under the chin. It was Gray Brother, one of his wolf brothers. He told Mowgli that he would bring all the news of the jungle to him.

The following months were very busy ones for Mowgli. He had to learn the ways of men, like wearing clothes, dealing with money and working in the fields. He got very angry when the village children made fun of him because he couldn't say words properly or play their games.

Mowgli listened to the village gossip and tried not to laugh at the silliness of it. Buldeo, the village hunter, told everyone that the tiger which had taken Messua's child was really the ghost of a wicked money-lender who limped. "It's true," he said, "because the tiger also limps. His tracks prove it!"

"What rubbish!" said Mowgli. "The tiger limps because he is lame, not because he's a ghost!"

"Oh, is that so, jungle brat?" answered Buldeo. "Well if you're so clever capture his hide. The Government offers a big reward."

MOWGLI'S REVENGE!

Mowgli was sent to tend the buffalo herd. He met Gray Brother there, who warned him that Shere Khan was looking for him, and that he was resting in the great ravine.

"I've an idea how to kill Shere Khan," said Mowgli. "I'll take the animals to the head of the ravine and then sweep down and surprise him. I must split the herd into two lots. Can you help?"

"Not alone," said Gray Brother, "but I've brought a wise helper."

It was Mowgli's old friend, Akela!

Soon all was ready, and the herd, bulls in one group and cows and calves in another, was led to the ravine. The sleepy, well-fed tiger was trapped.

Mowgli gave the order – and the herd charged. Shere Khan heard the thunder of hooves and bellowed in terror. Mowgli, on the back of Rama, the great herd bull, winded his enemy – and soon it was too late for the feared tiger as he was trampled to death by a thousand hooves.

"Let's skin him quickly!" said Mowgli.

Buldeo came running when he heard what had happened. Gray Brother and Akela left as soon as they saw him.

"What's this?" he asked angrily. "You, a child, skinning a huge tiger! It's the lame tiger, too. Well, perhaps I'll forget you let the herd loose. . . I'll take the skin and get the reward of a hundred rupees. I might give you one rupee."

Mowgli would have none of this, but Buldeo wouldn't leave him in peace.

"Akela, this man torments me!" Mowgli called into the distance.

Akela appeared from nowhere and pounced on Buldeo, pinning him to the ground. He lay still, too afraid to move. "What kind of magic boy is this, who can order a wolf about?" he asked himself.

Mowgli chuckled, "Let him go, Akela!"

Later, as he neared the village, Mowgli saw a group of angry villagers waiting for him.

"Go away, jungle-demon! Go back to the jungle, wolf's cub!" they cried.

Poor Mowgli sighed, "I had to leave the jungle because I'm a man – now I must leave here because you say I'm a wolf."

Messua ran to him crying, "I don't believe you're a demon. I know you avenged my son's death by killing the tiger, but go now, or they'll kill *you*."

So Mowgli returned to Mother Wolf's cave. "They have cast me away, Mother, but I've kept my word and brought Shere Khan's hide!"

Mother Wolf's eyes glowed with pride and happiness.

Mowgli laid the hide on Council Rock. The wolves saw it. They had no leader and were suffering badly, fighting and falling into traps.

"Lead us again, Akela!" they cried. "Lead us, man-cub!"

"Man pack and wolf have cast me out," said Mowgli. "I will hunt alone now."

"We will hunt with you," said his four wolf brothers.

And so Mowgli began his life in the jungle again.

Years later, Mowgli left the jungle once more. But in the meantime he had many more exciting adventures and learned much more about the ways of the jungle.

One year, the rains failed and all the jungle creatures searched for water. Another time, Mowgli rescued Messua and her husband, who were held captive as punishment for being kind to him when he came to their village.

In time, Father and Mother Wolf died, and so did brave, old Akela.

Finally Mowgli realised he must return to man, this time not because the jungle had cast him out.

"Man goes to man at last," said Kaa, the snake.

"Take your own trail," said faithful old Baloo. "But don't forget all I taught you. The jungle is yours to call on for help always."

Bagheera killed a bull, as he had so long before, when Mowgli was a baby. "All debts are paid now," he said. "Remember, I love you."

Mowgli sobbed and embraced his two old friends.

Gray Brother, the wolf, sniffed the air. "From now on, we all follow our own trails," he said.

First published in this abridged version by Carnival in 1988.

Carnival is an imprint of
the Children's Division, part of
the Collins Publishing Group,
8 Grafton Street, London W1X 3LA

Illustrations © Diana Catchpole, 1988

Printed and bound in Great Britain by
PURNELL BOOK PRODUCTION LIMITED
A Member of BPCC plc